Abigail
the Breeze
Fairy

by Daisy Meadows

illustrated by Georgie Ripper

Join the Rainbow Magic Reading Challenge!

Read the story and collect your fairy points to climb the Reading Rainbow online. Turn to the back of the book for details!

This book is worth 5 points.

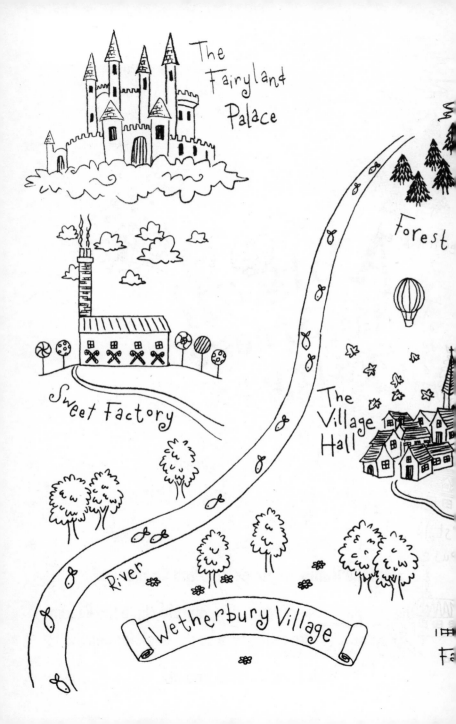

The Weather Fairies

Dedicated to the real fairies who
make my garden grow.

Special thanks to
Sue Bentley

ORCHARD BOOKS

First published in Great Britain in 2004 by Orchard Books
This edition published in 2016 by The Watts Publishing Group

3 5 7 9 10 8 6 4 2

© 2016 Rainbow Magic Limited.
© 2016 HIT Entertainment Limited.
Illustrations © Georgie Ripper 2004

HiT entertainment

A CIP catalogue record for this book is available from the British Library.

ISBN 978 1 40834 859 8

Printed in Great Britain by CPI Group (UK) Ltd, Croydon CR0 4YY

The paper and board used in this book are made from wood from responsible sources

Orchard Books
An imprint of Hachette Children's Group
Part of The Watts Publishing Group Limited
Carmelite House, 50 Victoria Embankment, London EC4Y 0DZ

An Hachette UK Company
www.hachette.co.uk
www.hachettechildrens.co.uk

Jack Frost's
Ice Castle
een Wood
Mrs. Fordham's Cottage
The Park
Willow Hill
The
Museum
The High St.
sty's
use
Fields
N
W
E
S
d
Mudhole

Goblins green and goblins small,
I cast this spell to make you tall.
As high as the palace you shall grow.
My icy magic makes it so.

Then steal Doodle's magic feathers,
Used by the fairies to make all weathers.
Climate chaos I have planned
On Earth, and here, in Fairyland!

Contents

The Adventure Begins   9

Cake Chaos!   23

Goblin Discovered   33

Up, Up and Away!   45

Flying High   59

Bright and Breezy   65

The Adventure Begins

"I'm so glad I could come and stay with you!" Rachel Walker said happily as she sat with her friend, Kirsty, in the garden. The sun shone brightly on the neat green lawn and pretty flowering bushes.

"Me too," agreed Kirsty Tate, smiling. "And it's very exciting to see the fairies again!"

Kirsty and Rachel had met while on holiday with their parents and they'd had a fairy adventure. They had found all the Rainbow Fairies and helped them bring the colour back to Fairyland, after Jack Frost had cast a nasty spell to banish them.

Now Jack Frost was causing more trouble in Fairyland. He had ordered his goblin servants to steal the seven magic feathers from Doodle, the fairy cockerel. Doodle was in charge of the weather in Fairyland, but without his magic tail feathers, he was powerless! Fairyland's weather would be topsy-turvy until Rachel and Kirsty could help the Weather Fairies recover all of Doodle's stolen feathers.

"I hope we find another magic feather today," said Rachel. She and Kirsty had already helped Crystal the Snow Fairy return the Snow Feather to Doodle.

The goblins were hiding around Kirsty's hometown of Wetherbury. And they had been up to mischief – using the magic weather feathers to conjure up some very unusual and troublesome weather in the country village.

Kirsty looked anxious. "We need to find the six other feathers," she said. "Or poor Doodle will be stuck on top of our barn forever!" She glanced up at the roof of the old wooden barn where Doodle was perched.

Here in the human world, without his magic, the magnificent fairy cockerel was just a rusty metal weather-vane.

Just then, a bush near the garden gate began to rustle. Kirsty and Rachel could see its pink flowers jiggling. Kirsty caught her breath.

"Do you think there's a goblin in that bush?" she whispered.

"Yes! I can see it moving," gasped Rachel. She felt nervous at the thought of facing another goblin. They were much scarier since Jack Frost had cast a spell to make them bigger.

"Come on!" Kirsty said, setting off across the lawn. "He might have one of Doodle's feathers."

Rachel followed her.

An angry yowl came from the middle of the bush. Rachel and Kirsty looked at each other in alarm.

Suddenly, two cats shot out and chased each other into the barn.

"Oh!" Kirsty exclaimed, and she and Rachel laughed with relief.

Kirsty's mum appeared at the front door. "There you are, Kirsty," she smiled. "Would you and Rachel like to go to the village fête and give your gran some support in the Cake Competition? She's hoping to win this year."

Kirsty and Rachel looked at each other. "We'd love to," Kirsty replied. "Gran makes the best cakes," she added.

Mrs Tate laughed. "Yes, she does. But you'd better hurry if you want to get there before the judging starts."

A few minutes later, the girls were hurrying down Twisty Lane towards the High Street. It was a beautiful day. Skylarks soared in the cornflower blue sky and wild flowers – like tiny jewels – dotted the hedgerows. As they drew near to a thatched cottage with a pretty garden full of roses and honeysuckle, a sharp gust of wind blew a shower of petals onto the pavement.

Then, a large white envelope landed at Kirsty's feet. "Where did that come from?" she murmured, and gasped as more letters came spinning and whirling towards her.

"The wind's really picked up," Rachel commented, stooping to pick up some of the letters.

"Hey! Come back!" called a voice. A postman was running towards them, chasing the envelopes that had been caught by the breeze.

The girls picked up the fallen letters
and handed them to the postman who
stuffed them back into his sack.

"Thanks," he grinned. "This wind's
blowing something fierce. Listen, it's
even catching at the church bell now!"

He went off to deliver his letters as
Kirsty and Rachel hurried on towards
the fête, listening to the church bell
clanging in the breeze.

The wind seemed to be getting
stronger and stronger, and when they
arrived at the fête, they saw that it was
causing havoc. Strings of bunting had
come loose and were blowing in the
wind like kite-tails. Three marquees
strained against their guy ropes as they
billowed and swayed. And several

stallholders were fighting to stop
their goods blowing away.

With a loud snap, the side of a tent
tore free from its ropes and began
flapping wildly. Some men ran over to
tie the canvas down. "Never known
wind like this in the height of summer,"
one of them complained.

As the girls set off in search of the Cake Competition, Kirsty noticed a small boy struggling to hold on to a yellow balloon. Suddenly, the wind whipped it out of his hand and sent it bobbing away across the grass.

"My balloon!" sobbed the boy.

"We'll catch it!" called Kirsty, already giving chase.

Rachel ran after her friend. "There's something very strange about this wind!" she shouted.

"I know," puffed Kirsty, jumping for the balloon's string. "Do you think it could be magic?"

Rachel nodded. And the girls looked at each other, their eyes shining with excitement.

Cake Chaos!

Kirsty and Rachel caught the balloon and took it back to its little owner who was standing outside one of the marquees. When he saw it, the boy's face lit up. "My balloon!" he beamed. "Thank you."

"You're welcome," Kirsty replied.

Just then she heard a familiar voice.

"Hello, Kirsty," called a plump, jolly-looking lady, as she bustled over to join the girls.

"Hi, Gran," Kirsty said. She turned to Rachel. "This is my dad's mum, Grandma Tate," she explained.

"Hello, Mrs Tate," said Rachel. She glanced at the huge cake tin that Kirsty's gran was holding. "Is that your entry for the competition?"

Kirsty's gran nodded. "It's chocolate fudge gateau," she said. "That grumpy Mrs Adelstrop always wins. But I think I'm in with a chance this year."

"Who's Mrs Adelstrop?" Rachel inquired.

Just then, another woman with a cake tin pushed rudely past. "Out of my way!" she demanded. "This wind is dreadful!" And with that she disappeared inside the marquee.

"I expect you've guessed who that was," whispered Kirsty's gran.

"Mrs Adelstrop!" chorused the girls.

"Right first time," said Gran with a laugh. "Well, I must dash." And she followed Mrs Adelstrop into the tent.

"Good luck," called Rachel.

"Shall we go inside, too?" Kirsty suggested. "The goblin with the Breeze Feather must be somewhere nearby. He might be hiding in the tent."

Rachel nodded and the girls wandered into the marquee. A tall, thin man with a notepad stood behind a table full of scrumptious-looking cakes.

Mrs Adelstrop smiled confidently as she placed an enormous lemon cake on the table.

"That looks pretty good," Kirsty whispered, noticing the sugared lemon slices on top.

Kirsty's gran took out her chocolate fudge gateau. Layers of chocolate sponge and butter cream filling were topped with icing and chocolate leaves. Mrs Adelstrop's smile wavered as she saw it.

"Wow! That's Gran's best cake ever!" Kirsty exclaimed happily.

"It looks delicious," Rachel agreed.

But as Mrs Tate stepped forwards to place her cake on the table, a ferocious gust of wind blew in through the marquee entrance. A length of coloured bunting snaked into the tent and tangled itself around her legs.

Mrs Tate stumbled and the cake flew out of her hands. It sailed through the air and landed – splat – right in the judge's face!

Kirsty's gran looked horrified.
"Oh, how dreadful! Look at the poor
judge," she whispered to the girls.
"And there go my chances of winning
the Cake Competition this year!" she
added sadly.

"What an awful accident," said Mrs
Adelstrop loudly. Kirsty thought she was
trying not to look pleased.

The judge stood there, covered in chocolate and icing, as everyone rushed to help him clean up. All around was the sound of rattling crockery and flapping canvas as the fierce wind battered at the marquee.

"The wind's getting worse," whispered Rachel. "See if the goblin is hiding under the table."

Kirsty lifted a corner of the tablecloth and peeped underneath, but there was no sign of a goblin.

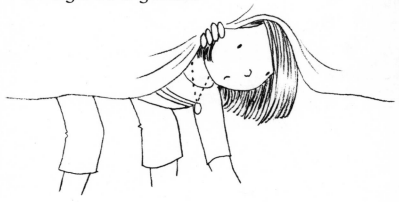

Rachel glanced around the marquee, looking for other possible goblin hiding places. Her eyes fell on a pretty fairy decoration, perched on top of a cake. Suddenly, she gasped. The tiny fairy was giving her a cheeky wave!

Goblin Discovered

The fairy's bright green eyes sparkled
with laughter. She wore a pretty yellow
top and a matching skirt with a little
green leaf near the hem. Her long
golden-brown hair was tangled and
windswept and she held an emerald
green wand with a shining golden tip.
Little bursts of coppery leaves swirled

33

from the tip of her wand.

Rachel's eyes widened. "Kirsty! Over here!" she whispered.

Kirsty hurried over. "It's Abigail the Breeze Fairy," she said delightedly. She and Rachel had met Abigail and all the Weather Fairies in Fairyland.

"Hello, Rachel and Kirsty!" Abigail said, and twirled in the air in a cloud of gold–green dust and tiny bronze leaves.

"Thank goodness we've found you. We think there's a goblin nearby," said Rachel.

Abigail's tiny face paled. "Goblins are nasty things — so big and scary — but we have to find this one," she said bravely, "before he does any more mischief with the Breeze Feather." She fluttered her glittering wings and swooped onto Rachel's shoulder to hide underneath her hair.

"Well, the goblin isn't in this marquee," said Kirsty. "Let's go outside and check the stalls."

"Good idea," Rachel agreed, and the two friends left the marquee, struggling to make headway against the blustery wind. They hadn't got far when there was a loud creaking noise, and suddenly the marquee behind them collapsed! The girls saw Kirsty's gran rushing to help others who were crawling out from beneath the canvas.

"Oh, what a mess!" said Rachel.

"At least it doesn't look as if anyone's hurt," Kirsty pointed out.

The wind moaned loudly through a spinny of oak trees standing nearby. The branches thrashed to and fro in the gale, and clouds of green leaves rained down.

Abigail's tiny mouth drooped. "Poor trees. It's too soon for them to lose their leaves," she said sadly.

"This is more goblin mischief!" fumed Kirsty. "If he keeps using the Breeze Feather, he'll make all the trees bare."

Quickly, the girls searched the tents and some of the stalls, but they didn't have any luck at all.

Then, Kirsty noticed a dog barking. "It's Twiglet," she said, pointing at an adorable Jack Russell puppy beside the Tombola stall. "His owner is one of our neighbours, Mr McDougall."

"We haven't searched the Tombola yet," Rachel said. "Let's go and check for goblins."

The girls hurried over. "Hello," Kirsty greeted her neighbour.

"Hello, lass," said Mr McDougall. "I reckon Twiglet doesn't like this windstorm."

Kirsty nodded. She bent down to
stroke Twiglet and the puppy jumped
up from beside his empty food bowl. He
wagged his tail and wiggled his little
body. Kirsty stroked his soft,
floppy ears. "You're
gorgeous," she smiled.

"What's that?"
Rachel asked,
pointing to a torn
piece of material
in Twiglet's mouth.

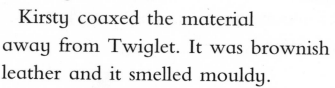

Kirsty coaxed the material
away from Twiglet. It was brownish
leather and it smelled mouldy.

Rachel and Kirsty peered at it closely.

"I'm sure I've seen something like it
before," Rachel said thoughtfully. "I
wonder where Twiglet got it from."

Suddenly, Twiglet began barking again. He was staring up at the sky and jumping up and down.

"That's odd," said Mr McDougall. "He keeps doing that."

"Maybe he's hungry?" suggested Rachel.

Mr McDougall shook his head. "Can't be, lass. His dish is empty. He must have bolted his food when I wasn't looking."

Twiglet snapped and growled crossly, still looking upwards. The girls and Abigail followed the puppy's gaze.

"Look at that!" Rachel pointed to a hot-air balloon floating in the sky above the fête. The balloon was striped red and orange and a large basket hung below it. The fierce wind sent leaves and bits of paper whirling around it, but the balloon itself seemed to hang almost stationary in mid-air. A bright spurt of flame shot from the burner to heat the air in the balloon and keep it aloft.

"That's odd," said Kirsty. "It doesn't seem to be affected by the wind at all!"

"Yes," Rachel agreed. "How can it be so still with the wind raging all around it?"

Abigail gave an excited cry. "The goblin must be hiding in it!" she exclaimed. "Only the magic Breeze Feather could protect the balloon from the wind like that."

Kirsty's eyes widened. "So we've found the goblin, at last," she said. "But he's way up in the sky!"

Up, Up and Away!

"How are we going to get up there?" Rachel asked.

"Easy!" Abigail told her. "We use fairy magic!"

The girls immediately reached for their shining golden lockets full of magic fairy dust. They had been special gifts from Titania, the Fairy Queen. A pinch

of the dust would turn the girls into
fairies and another would turn them
back to humans again.

Rachel sprinkled herself
with sparkling fairy
dust, then laughed
with delight as she
shrank to fairy size.
The grass was as tall
as she was, and the
buttercups now seemed as big as trees!

Kirsty did the same,
and twisted round
to look at her
silvery wings.
"Hurrah! I'm
a fairy again!"

"We must hurry!"
Abigail said, zooming into the air.

She was quickly followed by Kirsty
and Rachel.

The higher Abigail and the
girls flew, the more the
wind tore at them
and tried to blow
them off course.
Kirsty and Rachel
soon felt their
wings tiring.

"Fly in my
path," Abigail
urged the girls.
"You'll find it easier."

Rachel and Kirsty did as
she said and found it was less of
a struggle to follow the experienced
flying fairy. Abigail seemed to forge
an invisible path through the sky.

Gradually, they drew nearer and nearer to the balloon's basket.

"We were right. Look!" gasped Kirsty.

An ugly face peered over the edge of the basket. It was a goblin with pointed ears and a big, lumpy nose.

"He's a very big goblin," said Abigail nervously.

"I don't think he's seen us yet," Rachel whispered. "Let's creep up behind him."

The goblin was staring at Twiglet who was still barking down below.

"Ha, ha! Silly little doggy. You can't catch me!" he sneered. Kirsty and Rachel heard the goblin's tummy rumble. It sounded like mud being stirred in a bucket. The goblin gave a huge rude burp and a blast of horrid, stinky breath gusted over Rachel, Kirsty, and Abigail.

"Ugh!" Abigail held her nose. "What a terrible smell!" complained Rachel. "Whatever has that goblin been eating?"

"Can't catch me, doggy!" taunted the goblin, jumping up and down and waving a shining bronze feather.

A strong gust of wind swept Twiglet off his feet. The puppy tumbled over, got up again, and shook his head crossly. Then he looked up and began barking even more loudly.

The goblin jumped
back, looking a little
alarmed. Then he
recovered. "I'm safe
up here!" he said to
himself, and laughed.

Rachel felt puzzled. The goblin's
afraid of Twiglet, she thought. I
wonder why.

"He's holding the Breeze Feather!"
snapped Abigail. Her leaf-green eyes
flashed with anger.

"Yes. And he's using it to tease poor
Twiglet!" said Kirsty. "What a cheek!
We have to get that feather back."

Rachel was thinking hard. "I've got a
plan," she told her friends. "Kirsty, you
land in the basket. Then Abigail can
make you big and the two of you can

distract the goblin while I fly up and turn off the balloon's burner. The balloon will sink, and we'll have a better chance of getting the feather back once that goblin's grounded."

"It's a good idea," said Abigail. "But Kirsty and I will be very close to the goblin. Can you be quick, Rachel?"

"I will," Rachel promised.

"Here I go," Kirsty said. She checked

that the goblin wasn't looking and then fluttered up and over the lip of the basket. Abigail hovered next to her. With a wave of her wand, she turned Kirsty back to her normal size.

The goblin's eyes bulged as big as golf balls when he saw Kirsty. "Who are you?" he demanded.

"I'm Kirsty, a friend of the Weather Fairies," Kirsty declared firmly.

"And I'm Abigail the Breeze Fairy," Abigail added in her soft, musical voice.

The goblin glared at Abigail. "Boo!" he shouted, and lunged at her.

Abigail fluttered away in alarm and
the goblin snorted with laughter.

Behind the goblin's back, Kirsty saw
Rachel turning off the burner. So far so
good, she thought. The goblin hasn't
noticed Rachel.

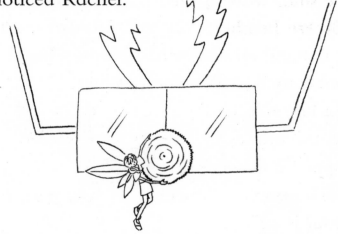

The goblin turned and scowled
at Kirsty. "Get off my balloon!"
he roared.

"That's not very polite," Kirsty said
calmly.

"Don't care!" snapped the goblin. He looked at Abigail slyly. "I know what you want and you shan't have it!" he said, waving the Breeze Feather.

A huge gust of wind rocked the basket. Kirsty clung to the side as it tipped dangerously.

The goblin sniggered. "Too windy for you, is it?"

"Your balloon's sinking," Kirsty told him.

"Codswallop!" sneered the goblin. Then he looked over the edge of the basket. "Oo-er!"

Below them, but getting nearer all the time, Twiglet barked and growled. The goblin's big nose twitched nervously.

Kirsty noticed a big rip in his leathery robe and remembered the piece of material in Twiglet's mouth. "Why are you afraid of the puppy?" she asked.

The goblin looked shifty. "I might have eaten his dinner," he replied sulkily.

No wonder his breath is so stinky! thought Kirsty.

"Now, tell me why this balloon's sinking!" demanded the goblin fiercely. "Or I'll wave the Breeze Feather and tip you out – like this!"

The basket rocked back and forth. Kirsty's heart pounded, but she clung on to the side. The goblin hardly moved, even though the basket shook and wobbled. He was perfectly balanced on his big broad feet. He brandished the Breeze Feather again, making the basket rock more than ever.

Kirsty reached anxiously for her fairy locket. Would she have time to use the fairy dust if she fell?

Flying High

"There's too much weight on board!
That's why we're sinking," said Abigail.

The goblin glared at Kirsty. "You're
too heavy. Get out!" he ordered.

Quick as a flash, Kirsty sprinkled
herself with fairy dust from her locket
and fluttered out of the goblin's way.

"We're still sinking!" the goblin

exclaimed in alarm. Suddenly, his ugly face brightened. "But I don't need these heavy sandbags. They just help the balloon to land," he said. And he grabbed the sandbags that hung around the edge of the basket and heaved them over the side. To his dismay, the balloon continued to sink lower and lower.

"What shall I do?" he wailed.

Abigail put her hands on her hips. "You'll have to throw out that feather!" she told the goblin firmly.

"Shan't!" snapped the goblin. "It's mine, and I'm keeping it! Besides, it's far too light to make any difference."

Kirsty and Rachel hovered behind Abigail. Would she be able to persuade the goblin to get rid of the feather?

"It's a lot heavier than you think," Abigail said craftily.

The goblin scowled. "What do you mean?"

"A kilo of feathers weighs just the same as a kilo of rocks, you know," she replied.

Kirsty and Rachel laughed softly. They knew that a kilo of anything weighs just the same as a kilo of anything else! But goblins are foolish, and the girls guessed that Abigail was hoping to confuse this one.

The goblin blinked and scratched
his head.

On the ground below, Twiglet barked
and jumped up at the balloon. He
seemed a lot closer now.

"Argh! Don't let it get me!"
screamed the goblin.
And in desperation,
he flung the feather
out of the basket.
Abigail shot after it in
a blur of golden wings,
but the feather was caught
by the wind and swept away.

"Come on!" shouted Rachel, flying
after Abigail. Kirsty followed.

The fierce wind buffeted the girls.

"The wind's too strong. I can't fly!"
cried Rachel in panic.

The girls were tossed and tumbled around by the wind. They flapped their wings and tried to regain control, but it was no use. They were drifting further and further from the Breeze Feather, and they couldn't even see Abigail for all the leaves and rubbish swirling around them.

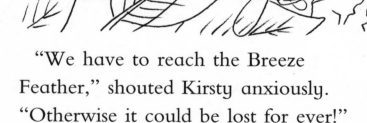

"We have to reach the Breeze Feather," shouted Kirsty anxiously. "Otherwise it could be lost for ever!"

Bright and Breezy

Suddenly, Kirsty and Rachel caught
sight of Abigail flying to their rescue.

"Don't worry about us," Kirsty
shouted above the wind.

"Just catch the Breeze Feather!"
Rachel yelled.

Abigail must have heard them
because she nodded firmly and sped off

after the feather again. She seemed
about to grab it when the wind
snatched it away from her. Rachel let
out a cry of despair, but then she saw
a rope of tiny golden leaves snake out
from Abigail's wand and wrap around
the Breeze Feather.

The tiny fairy pulled the feather
towards her and finally managed to
catch hold of it. She immediately
waved it in a complicated magic
pattern. "Wind, stop!" she ordered.

With a soft sigh, the roaring
wind died.

Kirsty and Rachel immediately found
that they could fly properly again.

Abigail flew to join them. "It's
wonderful to have the Breeze Feather
back safe and sound!" she said happily.

"What about the goblin?" asked
Kirsty.

Abigail frowned.
"Leave him to me!"
She pointed the
feather at the
hot-air balloon.
"Wind, blow!"
she commanded.
An enormous
puff of wind
rocked the balloon.

67

The goblin hung over
the basket. His face
looked greenish.
"I feel sick," he moaned.
"You shouldn't have eaten
Twiglet's dinner!" Rachel told him.
"I wish I hadn't now," replied the goblin
gloomily. "It wasn't very nice anyway!"
Abigail waved the Breeze Feather
a second time and the big red balloon
was blown high into the sky. The goblin's
moans faded, as the balloon flew out
of sight.

Kirsty, Rachel, and Abigail fluttered down to the fête and slid down the roof of one of the tents to the ground. Abigail waved her wand and Kirsty and Rachel grew to normal size.

They peeped out from behind the tent. People were rushing about setting their stalls to rights, and over at the Tombola, Twiglet was chewing contentedly.

"Mr McDougall has given Twiglet a chewstick," said Kirsty.

"I bet it tastes better than goblin's clothes!" laughed Rachel.

"Kirsty!" called Kirsty's gran.

Abigail quickly zoomed onto Kirsty's shoulder and hid beneath her hair.

"Gran!" Suddenly Kirsty remembered what had happened to her gran's cake. So why was her gran wearing such a broad grin?

"I won first prize!" said Mrs Tate, her eyes shining. "The judge said my cake was delicious. He couldn't help tasting it when it was all over his face!"

The girls were just congratulating Mrs Tate when Mrs Adelstrop stomped past, scowling.

Kirsty's gran chuckled. "She's won first prize for the last three years. It's time someone else had a chance!"

Rachel and Kirsty laughed. And only they heard the silvery giggling that came from under Kirsty's hair.

"Must go," said Gran. "My best friend, Mable, is hoping to win a prize for her marrow in one of the vegetable competitions!"

Kirsty and Rachel waved goodbye.

"We should go and give Doodle his magic feather back," said Kirsty.

The girls and Abigail headed home.

It was quiet and sunny now and a warm summer breeze gently rustled through the leaves in Twisty Lane. "Everything's back to normal," said Rachel happily.

Back at Kirsty's house, Abigail flew straight up to the barn roof and carefully put the Breeze Feather into Doodle's tail.

The weather-vane cockerel shimmered in a magic haze of gold. And then he fizzed into life and shook himself. Fabulous copper sparkles flew into the air, making Rachel and Kirsty gasp in wonder. Doodle's fiery feathers were magnificent.

Doodle shifted to settle the Breeze Feather properly into place, where it glimmered and glowed like polished bronze. Then he looked straight at Rachel and Kirsty. "Jack—" he squawked, and opened his beak as if to speak again, but the colour ebbed from his feathers. Doodle became a rusty old weather-vane once more.

"He's trying to tell us something," said Kirsty.

"Last time, he said 'Beware'," Rachel reminded Kirsty. "So now we have 'Beware Jack…' I wonder what he wanted to say next?"

Abigail floated down from the roof. "I don't know," she said. "But keep your eyes open. Jack Frost is always up to mischief."

"We will," Kirsty promised.

"Now I must fly back to Fairyland," Abigail said. "Thank you again, Rachel and Kirsty."

"Goodbye, Abigail!" Kirsty said, and Rachel waved.

Abigail's wings flashed, and with a swirl of tiny golden leaves, she was gone.

Rachel and Kirsty smiled at each other, enjoying their fairy secret.

"Five more magic feathers to find!" whispered Kirsty.

Meet the
Friendship Fairies

When Jack Frost steals the Friendship Fairies' magical objects, BFFs everywhere are in trouble! Can Rachel and Kirsty help save the magic of friendship?

www.rainbowmagicbooks.co.uk

Calling all parents, carers and teachers!
The Rainbow Magic fairies are here to help
your child enter the magical world of reading.
Whatever reading stage they are at, there's
a Rainbow Magic book for everyone!
Here is Lydia the Reading Fairy's guide to
supporting your child's journey at all levels.

Starting Out

1 Our Rainbow Magic Beginner Readers are perfect for first-time readers who are just beginning to develop reading skills and confidence. Approved by teachers, they contain a full range of educational levelling, as well as lively full-colour illustrations.

Developing Readers

2 Rainbow Magic Early Readers contain longer stories and wider vocabulary for building stamina and growing confidence. These are adaptations of our most popular Rainbow Magic stories, specially developed for younger readers in conjunction with an Early Years reading consultant, with full-colour illustrations.

Going Solo

3 The Rainbow Magic chapter books – a mixture of series and one-off specials – contain accessible writing to encourage your child to venture into reading independently. These highly collectible and much-loved magical stories inspire a love of reading to last a lifetime.

www.rainbowmagicbooks.co.uk

"Rainbow Magic got my daughter reading chapter books. Great sparkly covers, cute fairies and traditional stories full of magic that she found impossible to put down" – Mother of Edie (6 years)

"Florence LOVES the Rainbow Magic books. She really enjoys reading now" Mother of Florence (6 years)

Read along the Reading Rainbow!

Well done – you have completed the book!

This book was worth 1 star.

See how far you have climbed on the Reading Rainbow.
The more books you read, the more stars you can colour in
and the closer you will be to becoming a Royal Fairy!

Do you want to print your own Reading Rainbow?

1) Go to the Rainbow Magic website

2) Download and print out the poster

3) Colour in a star for every book you finish
and climb the Reading Rainbow

4) For every step up the rainbow,
you can download your very own certificate

There's all this and lots more at
rainbowmagicbooks.co.uk

You'll find activities, stories, a special newsletter
AND you can search for the fairy with your name!